PANDA books are for young readers
making their own way
through books.

O'BRIEN SERIES FOR YOUNG READERS

Where's Murphy?

Anna Donovan
Pictures by
Tatyana Feeney

THE O'BRIEN PRESS
DUBLIN

Celebrating the real Murphy

First published 2008 by The O'Brien Press Ltd,
12 Terenure Road East, Dublin 6, Ireland.
Tel: +353 1 4923333; Fax: +353 1 4922777
E-mail: books@obrien.ie
Website: www.obrien.ie

ISBN: 978-1-84717-081-1

British Library Cataloguing-in-Publication Data
A catalogue reference for this title is available from the British Library.

The O'Brien Press receives assistance from

1 2 3 4 5 6 7 8 9 10
08 09 10 11 12

Typesetting, layout, editing, design: The O'Brien Press Ltd
Printed and bound in the UK by CPI Group

Can YOU spot the panda
hidden in the story?

Murphy was
Rory's best friend.

Every morning,
Murphy came to
Rory's window
and barked and barked.

'Hi, Murphy,' Rory called.
The first thing he always did
was feed Murphy.

When Rory came
home from school
Murphy was always
waiting for him.

Then Rory got his tennis
racquet or his hurley.
He hit the ball
and Murphy raced after it.
Murphy brought the ball
back to Rory.

And Rory hit it again.
And again. And again.

If the ball went into the bushes,
Murphy dived in after it.

If it went behind the sheds,
Murphy raced in
behind the sheds.

Murphy would not stop
until he found the ball.
Murphy **loved** balls.

Rory and Murphy played
for hours in the summer.
In winter, they played
until it got dark.

Rory and **Murphy**.

Best, best friends.

But one day
when Rory came
home from school
Murphy wasn't there.

'Murphy!' called Rory.
Nothing.

Rory whistled.
No Murphy.
Rory shouted
at the top of his voice.
'**Murphy**! **Murphy**!'

Still no Murphy.

Rory ran into the house.
He dumped his school bag.
on the floor.
'Mam!' he called.
'Where's Murphy?'

'Murphy?' said, Mam.
'He was here when I got home.'
Mam and Rory were puzzled.

They walked all around
the neighbourhood
calling Murphy's name.
'Murphy! Murphy!'

They asked everyone they met
had they seen
a big, black Labrador dog?
Nobody had.

'Murphy's lost,'
Rory told Dad
as soon as he got home.

'What?' said Dad.
'We'll have to go
and look for him.'

So Mam and Dad and Rory called to all the neighbours. But nobody had seen the dog.

Where **was** Murphy?

'Maybe he just went
on a little adventure,'
said Mam.

'I hope he
comes back soon,'
said Rory.

‘Murphy is my
best, best friend
in the whole world.’

Nobody slept that night.
Sometimes Rory got up.
He looked out his window
at the moonlit night.
'Murphy!' he called
from time to time.
'Murphy!'

murphy

Mam and Dad
looked out too,
hoping to see the dog.

One time Dad thought
he heard a bark.
He ran downstairs
and opened the front door.
'Murphy!' he called.

But no Murphy came.

Next day Rory was very sad
as he left for school.

At school he told
all his friends
and his teacher
about the missing dog.

He told them
what Murphy looked like.
He showed them a photograph
of himself with Murphy.
'If any of you see
a dog like this,
please, please tell me,'
said Rory.

Rory's class made
special posters that morning.
They said:

That evening they went
with their parents
all over the town
and put up the posters.

Murphy did not come home
that night.

He did not come home
the next day.

Three nights
and three days passed.
There was still no sign
of Murphy.

‘Maybe somebody
has found him and
doesn’t know whose he is!’
said Mam.

‘Let’s hope so,’ said Dad.

'He should have a collar
with his name
and phone number,'
said Mam.

'Yes,' said Dad.
'We should have got that
before now.
I feel very bad about it.'

The very next day
Dad went to a shop
and got a collar.
It had a medal at the front.

Dad got Murphy's name
and phone number
written on the medal.
'When he comes back,'
Dad said, 'he'll wear this.'

He put it in Rory's bedroom.

Every day,
Dad and Mam and Rory
went for a long walk,
looking for Murphy.
They drove around too,
in case he had gone
really far.

But they never saw Murphy.

One day Dad made copies of
Murphy's photograph.
He made sixty copies.

That evening Rory and Dad
took them to lots
of pubs
and shops
and restaurants.

Everybody said
they would look out
for the dog.

The very next day
a call came.
'I saw a dog like yours,'
said the boy on the phone.

He told Dad
where he lived.
Mam and Dad and Rory
drove straight away
to the boy's house.

He took them to the place
where he had seen the dog.

The dog was sitting
outside a big house.
It was a big, black Labrador.
It looked very like Murphy.

Rory and Dad and Mam
stared at the dog.
Was it Murphy?
'Murphy?' called Rory.

The dog stood up.
He looked at Rory.
He raced over.
He barked.

It wasn't Murphy.

'That's not Murphy's bark,'
said Rory.
'And he's bigger than Murphy,'
said Dad.

'Poor Rory,' said Mam.
'I'm sure we'll find him, love.
We'll just keep
hoping and looking.'

Another call came
two days later.
It was a woman.
She told Mam where she lived.

'That's too far,' said Dad.
'Don't get your hopes up, Rory.'
They all got in the car again.

Rory was hoping and hoping
that it was Murphy.
'Please, please, please,
let it be him!'

It took Mam a long time
to find the woman's house.
Mam and Dad and Rory
knocked at the door.
They heard a loud bark.

'**That's Murphy**!' said Rory.

‘Are you sure?’ asked Mam.
‘Maybe it isn’t–’
The door opened
and a big black ball burst out.

It fell on Rory.
It **was** Murphy.

'Murphy, Murphy, Murphy,'
said Rory.
'**My Murphy**!
We've found you.'

Mam and Dad
had tears in their eyes.
Rory was shouting
and jumping with joy.

Murphy was leaping
all over the place
and barking his head off.

'Well,' said the woman
at the door,
'I'd say that's **your** dog,
all right!'

'It is!' said Rory.
'This is Murphy.
He's my best, best friend
in the whole world.
But **why** did he run away?'

'I think I know
what happened,'
said the woman.

'You **DO**?' said Rory.

'Well,' said the woman.
'Does Murphy like **balls**?'

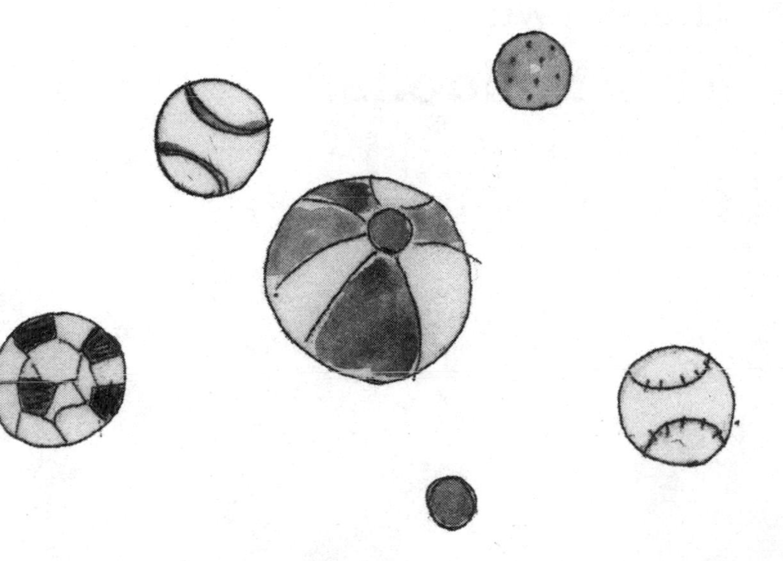

'Murphy **loves** balls,'
said Rory.

'Well,' said the woman again,
'it was a very windy day
when Murphy came here.
The sky was
full of **balloons**.'

'I think
Murphy followed
the balloons.'

'He was looking up
into the sky,' she said,
'and **forgot** where
he was going!'

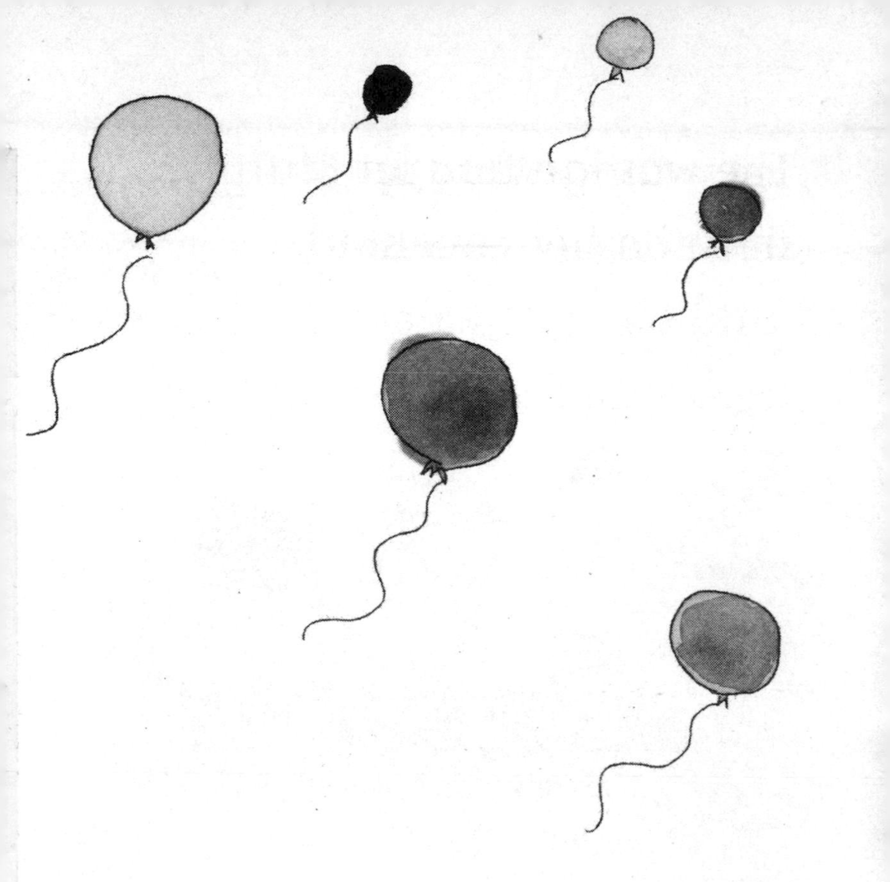

‘Then he couldn’t find
his way home,’ she said.
‘Poor Murphy,’ said Rory.
‘I’m so glad he found **you**.’

The woman had let Murphy sleep on her couch.

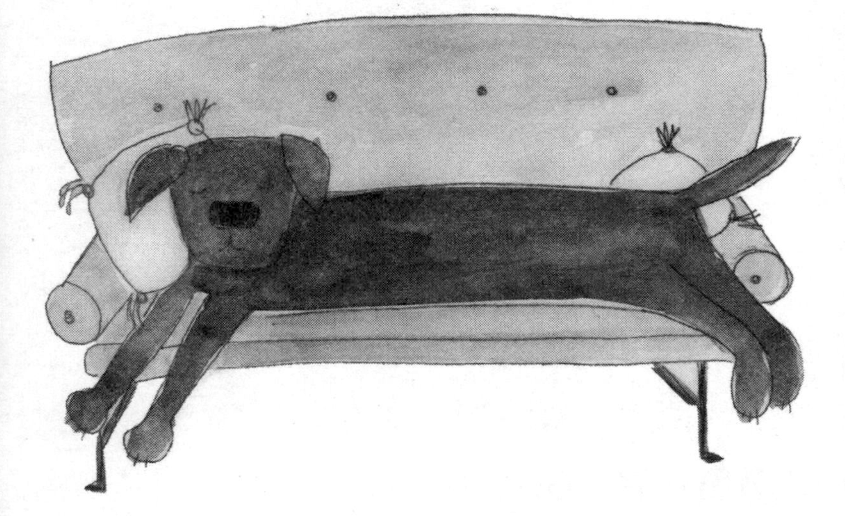

Then she saw the notice
with Murphy's photo
in a shop.
That's when she phoned.

'I'm going to miss him,'
she said.
'But I'm glad he has found
his **best**, **best friend**
in the whole world.'

Mam and Dad and Rory
thanked the woman
for looking after their dog
so well.

'I loved having him around,'
she said.
'But my cats were not
too happy.'

'I'll bring him back
to see you,'
promised Rory.

'Now Murphy has
another good friend –
forever.'